I AM READING

The Perfect Monster

SALLY GRINDLEY

Illustrated by
ERICA-JANE WATERS

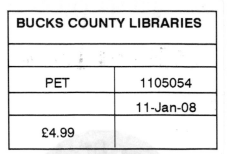

KINGFISHER
An imprint of Kingfisher Publications Plc
New Penderel House, 283-288 High Holborn
London WC1V 7HZ
www.kingfisherpub.com

First published by Kingfisher 2005
6 8 10 9 7 5

A CIP catalogue record for this book
is available from the British Library.

ISBN-13: 978 0 7534 1142 1

Printed in China
5TR/0707/WKT/SC/115MA

Contents

Chapter One

From the very first day of his life, Mungus
Bigfoot was THE PERFECT MONSTER.
When he was born, he screamed so
loudly – AAAAAAGH! – that all the
windows in the hospital broke. CRASH!
"What a perfect entrance!" everyone said.

When his mother
changed his nappies,
he always soaked her
– WEEEE!
"What a perfect shot!"
everyone said.

When aunties held their fingers out for him to suck, he bit them – EEEK! "What perfect teeth!" everyone said. His parents couldn't have been more proud.

When Mungus Bigfoot was two, he won
a prize for scaring old ladies at bus stops.

When he was three,
he won a competition
to find the loudest
GRRRR!

When he was four, he
came first in a contest
to see who could
throw their food
the furthest.

When he was five,
he went to school
and was declared
the dirtiest, smelliest
monster in his class.

When he was six,
he knew more rude
words than all of
his classmates put
together.

When he was seven, he was the youngest monster ever to pass his "Monster in the Cupboard" test.

When he was eight, he was awarded the
highest marks ever on his "Monster
under the Bed" test.

Every year, he was told, "Mungus
Bigfoot, you are THE PERFECT
MONSTER."

Chapter Two

Then, one day, Mungus Bigfoot was given a very special job.

"I want you to show Emily Twinkletoes how to be a good monster," said the Head Monster at his school.

Mungus was horrified.

"But Emily Twinkletoes is THE WORST
MONSTER EVER!" he protested. "She
won't even say boo to a goose!"

"If anyone can help her, you can," the Head Monster said. "She'll listen to you."

"I won't obey you," growled Mungus.

"For once, you will," ordered the Head Monster, "or you will be expelled."

Mungus Bigfoot couldn't believe his ears.
Expelled! He was THE PERFECT
MONSTER. They couldn't expel him!

Chapter Three

Emily Twinkletoes was put next to him in class.

"You're so perfect, Mungus Bigfoot," she whispered. "I wish I could be like you."

"Then try a bit harder," growled Mungus.

"I've tried, but I'm just no good at it," said Emily with a sigh.

"Throw this bag of flour at the teacher," said Mungus.

"Ooo, I couldn't," said Emily. "That would be naughty."

"You're supposed to be naughty," snapped Mungus. "Watch this."

He hurled the bag of flour and hit the
teacher full in the face – SPLAT!
"Who did that?" shouted the teacher.

"Emily Twinkletoes," Mungus replied.

"What a great shot!" said the teacher.

"Ten out of ten!"

"Oh, but it wasn't me," cried Emily.

"Shhh!" said Mungus. "Now, shout out the worst rude word you can think of."
Emily went bright pink. "Ooo, I couldn't," she said with a giggle.
"Shout it," growled Mungus.
Emily took a deep breath. "Poo!" she whispered.

Mungus gave her a nasty look, then he yelled out, "Stinkpongysmellobum!"

"Who said that?" demanded the teacher.

"Emily Twinkletoes," said Mungus.

"What a great rude word!" said the teacher. "Ten out of ten!"

"Oh, but it wasn't me," cried Emily.

Mungus felt like tearing his hair out.

At breaktime, Emily asked him to play hopscotch with her.

"Not blooming likely," said Mungus. "We're going to frighten the nursery monsters."

"Ooo, I couldn't do that!" squealed Emily.

At lunchtime, Emily asked him to play

skipping with her.

"Not blooming likely," said Mungus.

"We're going to throw tomatoes at the

dinner monsters."

"Ooo, I couldn't do that!" squealed
Emily.

"What can you do then?" groaned
Mungus.

"I know all my times tables," said
Emily, "and I can do joined-up writing,
and I can read all the words in the
dictionary, and I know how to be nice."

Mungus gasped with horror. "But that's terrible," he howled. "Your parents must be so ashamed of you."

"They are," nodded Emily. "But you're going to help me make them proud." Then she gave Mungus such a beautiful great big smile that he couldn't help smiling back.

Chapter Four

Over the next few weeks, Mungus tried
everything he could think of to turn
Emily into a better monster.

He taught her how to scream a really scary scream.

But instead of screaming, Emily taught him how to sing.

He taught her all the rude words he knew. But instead of saying them, Emily taught him how to spell them.

He showed her how to hide behind
bushes and jump out to frighten
passers-by. But instead of frightening
anyone, Emily showed Mungus how to
make a daisy-chain.

He showed her how to hide under a bed,
ready to scare a sleeping child.

But Emily snuggled up to him and fell
fast asleep.

The worst thing was that Mungus began to like Emily the way she was. "You're so different from any other monster I've ever met," he said.

"I know," she said with a giggle.

"It's terrible, isn't it? But you're helping

me change, aren't you, Mungus?"

Mungus made a face and mumbled,

"I think you might be changing me."

Emily looked shocked. "But that's awful!

You can't change, Mungus.

You're everybody's hero."

"And if I don't make you into a better

monster, I'll be expelled," Mungus sighed.

Emily looked even more shocked.

"I didn't know that," she whispered.

Chapter Five

The next day began with a lesson in
pulling faces.

"I want you to pull the nastiest face
imaginable," the teacher said to the class.

"I'm going to try really hard today,"
Emily whispered to Mungus.

Mungus looked at her beaming smile and
shook his head.

"You couldn't pull a nasty face," he said.

"You wait and see," grinned Emily.

One by one, the monsters pulled the worst
faces they could.

When it came to Mungus's turn, he pulled such a horrible face that all the other monsters cheered.

"What a truly horrible face!" cried the teacher. "Ten out of ten."

Then Emily Twinkletoes leapt to her feet.

"Look at this," she cried.

And she pulled such a terrible face that

all the other monsters cowered in their

boots.

"What a horrible, awful, nasty, foul, gruesome, terrible face!" cried the teacher. "One hundred out of one hundred!"

"I did it!" screamed Emily. "Did you see me, Mungus?"

Mungus nodded his head. "Well done, Emily," he said. But he looked very sad. Emily had pulled the worst face he had ever seen, but he didn't like her doing it.

During that day, Emily made the worst slime pie anyone had ever tasted.

She came top of the class in scary leaps off tables.

And she came top at making rude noises.

When she hurled a mud pie straight into
the Head Monster's face, he cheered and
patted Mungus on the back.

"Well done, Mungus," he said. "You've
turned Emily Twinkletoes into a perfect
little monster."

Instead of being pleased, Mungus felt

terrible. He walked sadly home.

Suddenly, he heard his name.

"Wait for me, Mungus."

Emily ran up to him and slipped her

hand into his.

"Thank you for helping me, Mungus," she said.

Mungus shook his head. "You were perfect the way you were and now I've spoiled you."

Emily looked very worried. "Was I too good at pretending to be bad?" she asked.

"What do you mean?" said Mungus.

"I forgot to tell you that I'm a brilliant actress," she grinned.

"You mean you haven't really changed?" asked Mungus.

"No, I haven't," Emily giggled.

"I have, though," sighed Mungus.

"That's terrible," said Emily solemnly.

And then she clapped her hands and gave him a great big hug. "You're more perfect than ever before," she smiled.

"You're my perfect monster."

About the Author and Illustrator

Sally Grindley is an award-winning author with many books to her name. She had a whale of a time writing *The Perfect Monster*.

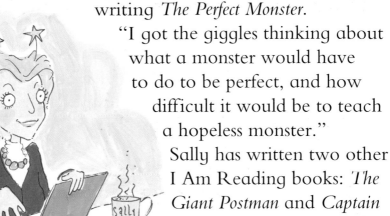

"I got the giggles thinking about what a monster would have to do to be perfect, and how difficult it would be to teach a hopeless monster."

Sally has written two other I Am Reading books: *The Giant Postman* and *Captain Pepper's Pets*.

Erica-Jane Waters paints lots of pictures, mostly for children's books. She says, "I'm a complete Mungus - I'm always covered in paint and occasionally throw food. In my spare time, I like getting muddy in my garden where I grow strange vegetables. Last year I grew green, warty pumpkins!"

Tips for Beginner Readers

1. Think about the cover and the title of the book. What do you think it will be about? While you are reading, think about what might happen next and why.

2. As you read, ask yourself if what you're reading makes sense. If it doesn't, try rereading or look at the pictures for clues.

3. If there is a word that you do not know, look carefully at the letters, sounds, and word parts that you do know. Blend the sounds to read the word. Is this a word you know? Does it make sense in the sentence?

4. Think about the characters, where the story takes place, and the problems the characters in the story faced. What are the important ideas in the beginning, middle and end of the story?

5. Ask yourself questions like:
Did you like the story?
Why or why not?
How did the author make it fun to read?
How well did you understand it?

Maybe you can understand the story better if you read it again!